Zack's Ch

©2019 by Stella Clark

All rights reserved. No part of this may be reproduced, distributed or transmitted in any form or by any means without prior written permission.

This is a work of fiction. Names, characters, places and incidents are a product of the author's imagination. Any resemblance to actual people, living or dead, or to businesses, events or locales is completely coincidental.

Chapter 1
Chapter 2
Chapter 3
Chapter 4
Chapter 5
Chapter 6
Chapter 7
Chapter 8
Chapter 9
Chapter 10
Chapter 11
Chapter 12
Chapter 13
Chapter 14
More Books by Stella Clark

Chapter 1

She glanced towards the dark window to listen.

There was the familiar snipping of their gardener, Jackson, cutting away at the hedges below. It would be the last trim of the year until spring returned to New York City. Their large home would soon be covered in snow. Then the holidays would be upon them. And then spring. And the heat.

It was an endless cycle that Della Prescott dreaded.

Every year was the same. There were the same seasons with few differences. There was the same house that she stayed in every day.

There were the same parties; one for her family and their friends, and one just for the family.

Everyone treated the double holidays like they were a special activity, a secret from the world.

They were a secret. But she wasn't the one giggling about them like everyone else did.

Her whole family tried to make the best of it.

But she knew. She knew because it was all her fault. She had known for as long as she could remember that her life was different, which forced her family to be different, which was all her fault.

Judy Hanson, the prettiest girl in New York City, had married the finest and richest man on the east coast, Donald Prescott. They had the biggest wedding New York had seen in over fifty years. It was the talk of the century. Apparently, it was still referred to in the newspapers for many reasons.

Everyone had expected a happy ever after future for them and the family they readily built. Except that the moment Judy Prescott held her first baby in her arms, something had gone terribly awry.

The baby girl had soft blonde hair with bold blue eyes. But there was something wrong. She wasn't perfect in the way that Judy Prescott had sworn her children would be.

Della could picture the moment perfectly.

"What happened?" Judy would have cried out. Her hair would have still looked perfect. The new mother would have been torn between protecting her in her arms and giving her back to be fixed. "What did you do to my child?"

Sitting at her armoire, Della sighed. It was a lovely little set, handmade just for her only thirteen years ago for her tenth birthday. Everything was perfect about the furniture except for the mirror. There was no mirror.

Her mother, the stunning Judy Hanson Prescott, had claimed she didn't need it. She was beautiful without having to appease her vanity. But most of all, she didn't want to make Della feel bad. That part had not been said, but the silence said enough.

"Miss?"

Della froze in her seat, realizing she had been tracing the birthmark on her cheek again. It was red and a little puffy, very distinctive and not something that she could hide.

Because she couldn't hide it, her parents thought hiding her away from the world would fix the problem.

"Yes, Hazel?" She forced herself to smile at the maid. "What is it?"

The young woman stepped into the room only to frown. "Your meal, Miss Della. You didn't eat again. Is everything all right?"

Her eyes dropped over to the table in the other corner of the room where the tray sat. "Oh." Della shrugged. "I'm fine. I'm just… Did my delivery come? The books? I was waiting on the new books about art. Did they arrive?"

The younger girl hesitated before shaking her head and picking up the tray. "I'm afraid not. Only two newspapers were delivered. Would you like to read those?"

She considered it before shaking her head. "No, thank you."

Hazel nodded and left. Della was left to her own devices as usual. She studied the dark shades on her window that kept the outside world from seeing her. It didn't help her see out very well. She wrinkled her nose. Then her stomach growled. Trying not to think about the world she had never been part of, now all Della could think about was the food that had just left the room.

"Hazel?" Della called over her shoulder.

But the young woman was gone.

Though she didn't have free reign of the world, she did have free reign of the house. Della brushed her long hair over her shoulders as she stood up and headed down the hall. There was the grand staircase to the right, but she didn't like that one. Her mother didn't like her going down that one, anyway. There was always the chance they might have an unexpected guest grace their halls. Instead, she preferred the servants' stairs to the left where she was less likely to be met.

She reached the back of the kitchen in seconds. Though she raised her voice to call for Hazel and see about finding something to eat at last, there were voices speaking that caused her to hesitate.

"But a stranger!" It was Lulu's loud southern voice, the newest of the maids. "You'd up and marry a man you never met?"

The short cook, Elsie Bell, answered softly. "I think so. Why not? It's not like there's a chance to meet any gents when we work all day. Don't you want to do something else with your life when you grow old? Just think of it.

Your own home. A husband to watch out for you."

"I don't know," Hazel sounded hesitant herself. "Leaving New York? It's home."

"But there's a whole world out there," Elsie sighed. "You said yourself you'd leave if you found the right opportunity."

Della decided she had listened long enough. "Leave? What, and leave me here on my own?" She tried to turn it into a joke, though it fell awkwardly off her tongue.

The maids jumped with guilty expressions on their faces. As she looked around, she was disappointed more to see that none of them would look her in the eye. She bit her lip and fiddled with her hair, tugging it in front of her cheek.

"It's nothing, Miss," Hazel started.

But she shook her head. "No, please. Go on. What are you talking about, marrying strangers? Let's have us some food, and you can tell me all about it."

That made the young girl brighten up. Hazel was a plump young woman who believed food solved all ills and worried about everything. She hurried into the pantry to find a snack as she explained what it meant to become a mail-order bride. The others followed her, filling in the details and offering their opinions.

It was a quaint idea.

The boredom and hole in her heart had lasted too long. By the time they finished their conversation, Della pulled Hazel aside with a plan that had begun to form in her mind. She couldn't stay trapped in her parents' home for the rest of her life, after all. There was a world out there that she wanted to see. Since her parents were too embarrassed by her existence, she knew she would have to take care of it herself.

Hazel acted as her intermediary since she already handled the mail. Having few others to put into her confidence, Della convinced the young maid to help her reply to several adverts for mail-order brides. At first, it was dreamy and thrilling.

And then there came a response from a rancher in Dawson, Montana that changed everything.

Chapter 2

The cold used to send a thrill down Zack Heston's spine. He liked the way the seasons changed and what came with it. Christmas was once his favorite time of year. For thirty years, he adored the fir trees and the way the world grew soft.

But since then, his heart had hardened, and it no longer held the same joy it once had.

"Papa?"

His gaze left the open window as it swung over to the little boy sitting at the table. Short brown hair and green eyes made him think of Ella. But it was Ross. Little Ross who was already eight years old. The boy could finally touch the ground with the tips of his toes while sitting around his chair. But now, he was swinging his feet beneath the seat as he stared back with an intense look.

Pulling himself back to the present, Zack managed a smile. "Yes, Ross? What is it?"

"Are we going to have Christmas this year?"

A lump formed in his throat. Closing the window, Zack turned to the table and set another piece of cheese on the boy's plate. "Of course. It comes every year. Why would you ask me that?"

The boy shrugged as he ate his cheese with both hands. "I don't know. It's just different now. That's all."

Zack knew exactly what he meant. There weren't words for the pain that clung tightly to his chest and weighed him down. Ella. His wife.

Ross's mother. She had been gone nearly two years. He thought the days would get easier with time, but he was still waiting for a sense of relief.

"I know," he managed at last. Taking a seat at the table across from his son, he tried to smile. Ross was still a child, and he deserved to enjoy the holidays. He still deserved a childhood. Zack slapped his hands against the table and tried to look energetic. "We'll go to your cousins' house to celebrate. You still like them, don't you?"

Ross chuckled sheepishly. "Yeah. They're fun. I like Bobby the most."

"Bobby is a smart kid," Zack nodded approvingly. Bobby was the oldest and the most responsible. If his son could follow in his nephew's footsteps, then all the better for everyone. "Good. Now, is there anything you want for Christmas?"

His son stared down at the last piece of cheese and shrugged. "I don't know."

But he did know. He just did that when he didn't want to say.

It was clear to his father that the boy was hiding something. Zack couldn't give up now. He nudged his son on the foot with his boot. "Come on, now. What is it? A wheelbarrow? A toy soldier? No, it's a horse, huh? I said you'd get one when you're ten."

"I know," the boy fiddled with the cheese but wouldn't eat it. Then he put it down and put on a serious face. Eight-year-old boys weren't supposed to have such sober expressions. But losing a mother could do that to a child.

The lump in Zack's throat grew even as he tried to ignore it. "Well?" He forced.

Ross took a deep breath. "I want a mother for Christmas." The cheese went in his mouth with a loud plop. It was a big piece so he couldn't talk. Because he didn't want to. He stared at the empty plate and waited.

His hands sat limp on the table between them. Zack wanted to retract them, but worried that his son would take that as a sign that he was angry or pulling away from him. He tried to breathe as he digested what the boy had just said. It was a basic enough concept. His son just wanted to be part of a family again.

But the simplicity of the truth didn't prevent the harsh pain that seared his heart.

***

The following Sunday, Zack confessed to his sister about what his son had said. Leah had married Robert Ganey twelve years ago when she was hardly seventeen. Robert had just bought the land next to Zack's cattle ranch. Though both men understood they should see each other as competition, they found themselves working side by side and frequently offered a helping hand instead.

"That poor boy," Leah murmured with a shake of her head. She blew a strand of her blonde hair away from her face after a sigh. "He's a child, Zack. Of course he wants a mother. Every day he goes to school, he sees the other children with their moms. He feels left out. He misses having a mother's love."

Leaning over the kitchen sink, it took all his strength not to bring the meatloaf up that

Leah had prepared everyone for supper. He knew he shouldn't have eaten too much. Zack closed his eyes as he imagined Ross running around the house looking for the present he knew he couldn't give his son.

"How can I disappoint him?" Zack groaned.

"Get married."

Robert walked over with the last couple of plates. It was the three adults in the kitchen now as the children ran around in the snow outside to enjoy the last of the sunlight. Leah muttered something under her breath to her husband as Zack tried to tune them out.

"It's only been two years," Leah hissed. "I told you we'd talk to him about it next year."

Her husband snorted loudly. "If Ross wants a mother, I'm sure Zack wants a wife. I'm not being cruel here, Zack. I'm just realistic. Now that I've had my good luck charm of a wife all these years, I can't imagine losing her. I can't run this house or my ranch without her. The fact you've gone this long on your own is a miracle. But that doesn't mean you have to do it alone."

Leah cleared her throat. "He's not alone. He has us, remember? Or me, at least."

"Hey," Robert frowned.

But Zack just shook his head. His heart hurt. Now, all he could see was his son's eventual disappointment. After all the hardships they had endured in the last couple of years, he'd do anything to make his boy happy again. Really happy. "Even if I wanted to get married again, I don't know what I would do. There aren't enough single women in town."

"That's why we'd send out a mail-order bride advert," Leah offered promptly.

She hadn't even hesitated. The woman had clearly put some thought into it.

So much so that she had him convinced before the sun had set and had an advert all prepared. Leah was the type of person to mother everyone, even if she was the younger of the two siblings. Zack didn't know how it happened but soon, he found himself exchanging missives to one particular young woman who had responded to his letters.

"Are you sure about this?" He asked when Leah closed up the most recent letter.

His sister nodded. "You're making the right decision. You may think of her as a friend if nothing else?"

It was an invitation for the young woman - his mail-order bride - to come out west. Though he spent several sleepless nights pondering if it was the right decision to make, especially around the holidays, Zack couldn't forget the hope in his son's eyes and eventually decided it was the right move.

But after the invitation was sent, he decided to send one final letter.

Just one more. A quick explanation. It would be a marriage, he explained to Della Prescott, but only one of convenience. His heart was too wounded to love another. There wasn't room to fit another wife in there.

Still, he would do his best. He would care for her as best he could and give her a safe, warm home. Hopefully that would be enough for everyone. Especially Ross.

Chapter 3

Della pulled the veil over her face with shaky hands as her carriage came to a stop.

She could hear the noise of people bustling about, moving and shouting around the train station. A whistle blew, and it made her jump. A hand touched her shoulder, and she turned to Hazel who looked at her in concern.

"It's all right," Della assured her breathlessly. "I'm all right."

That's what she had to tell herself, as well. That everything was good and that she was making the right decision. Even though she had spent a week repeating this in her mind, Della wasn't certain she had convinced herself it was the truth just yet.

But there was no time to spare. It was time for her to go.

"Thank you for all of your help," she told Hazel. "I'll write to you when I have arrived. Please make certain that my parents find the letter on my pillow, would you?" And then she put on her bravest smile. "How do I look?"

The young maid fixed the netted veil near her ear and ran a hand over her shoulder before nodding. In the last couple of weeks, Della liked to think they had become nearly friends. "Like a queen, Miss Della. You're terribly brave for doing this. I'll be looking for your letter and will write you a response of how your family responds."

Overcome with emotion, Della wrapped her arms around the young woman. "Thank you," she whispered, "for everything."

Another whistle sounded, and she took it as a sign that it was time for her to go. Her heart pounded furiously. Della was helped out of the carriage, and Hazel guided her to the steps of the train. It was a mad house of chaos everywhere she looked. The entire street was crowded with people boarding and people staring.

She couldn't help but stare in fascination at everyone. How could they live like this? It was hard to imagine living life every day surrounded by so many people. Though her family spoke often of such congestion, she'd hardly ever left the family grounds and had assumed they were making up stories and lies for her. Never had she been free to mill around in the lane that was filled with people shoulder to shoulder.

When the strangers bumped into her, she faltered. Hazel wrapped a hand around her elbow after she had jumped for the tenth time. It was most crowded, Della decided, and she was relieved when they reached the train and she was helped onboard. Hazel handed over her luggage and offered a small wave.

Then Della was alone.

Taking a deep breath, she swallowed and took her two bags into the car where she found the compartment that Hazel had helped her reserve. It was a tiny room, but she had it all to herself. Her heart was pounding as she took a seat and tried to grasp what she had just done. Everything had fallen into place so quickly that she worried she wasn't holding all the pieces.

Her parents were out for the day with their friends, so she had easily left undetected. She had been slowly packing things into her bags for the last week with Hazel's help. There had been several purchases to make, several plans to organize. Della hadn't had a full night's sleep in nearly a month, and she could feel the exhaustion seeping into her bones.

A whistle sounded. The floor beneath her began to move. Della gasped as she fell back against the bench. Her breathing grew short and loud, overwhelmed with everything that had just happened.

It was rare for her to be somewhere new, let alone not with her parents or a maid. For a minute, she tried to both breathe and swallow the panic rising in her throat. Closing her eyes, Della focused on gathering her breath. These moments of panic had come often enough to her as a child. She thought of Elsie, the cook, humming to her back in those days to give her the courage to recover. Della tried to remember the words.

"Morning stars are growing light, let's say farewell unto the night," she whispered to herself with her eyes tightly closed. "And sing in joy for all is well."

After another verse, she started to feel better. Della grew used to the repetitive movements of the train. It was just like any other carriage that she had ever ridden. And then she gathered her courage and swallowed the fear.

This was what she wanted. New York City had nothing there for her. She was finally going to escape and go somewhere. It was a dream that she was making come true.

This slowly dawned on Della what she had just accomplished. After a moment, she laughed in amazement.

She had done it. She had escaped New York; she had escaped the eternal confinement her parents had kept her in. For the first time in her life, she was free. Della laughed, clapping her hands before settling down. She was no longer trapped in her house with nothing but books for her friends. Now, she was on her way to a man who wanted her.

In her fourth letter, she had finally gathered the courage to explain she had a birthmark. A large one on her face that didn't look pretty, but it didn't prevent her from doing anything. She had already described her long blonde hair and large blue eyes that were gifts from her mother. Telling him about the birthmark had terrified her. She had followed it up with her fifth letter where she asked how much he cared about people's looks. Though he never addressed her birthmark, he had eventually responded to say that looks meant little for it was the heart that mattered.

Della slowly began to relax as her journey continued.

There was so much to think about. She tried to imagine what he looked like. Zack Heston. He mentioned he was tall and thick shoulders along with blue eyes and blond hair himself. She wondered if he was handsome. Though the man had mentioned he was older, she didn't mind. He had sounded like a good man, and that was what mattered most.

It wasn't until she arrived in Dawson, Montana that Della wondered if she would really find love.

Her heart pounded as she stepped out into the sunlight. Carrying her bags off the train, Della mustered all of her courage to look up. She had put the netted veil back across her face but knew she couldn't keep it on forever. She only prayed that he was still willing to look past it into his heart.

All she wanted was someone brave enough to want her. And she was more than ready to return the favor.

Chapter 4

Zack couldn't stop pacing.

He had tried to stand still. But then his legs started dancing, and he kept rubbing his hands. Nothing seemed to help. It felt like there were ants all over him, and he couldn't stop moving. His heart thumped loudly, and he considered again just walking away.

But he could just imagine Ella's frown for such bad manners.

"This was a mistake," he mumbled under his breath to respond to the image of his wife in his mind. He shook his head and fiddled with the hat on his head. "A big one."

Then Ross's sober face came to mind. His boy had lost weight and a lot of laughter in the last couple of years. His little man had been struggling. At first, there had been nightmares. There were weeks on end where Zack had to go wake him up every night to stop the cries. Then Ross had stopped wanting to play with his toys or read.

Grief had drained them both of energy.

While Zack didn't expect his own life to get any better, he wanted more for Ross. The boy needed someone else who could give him the time and attention he needed to thrive. Ross deserved better. Though he had considered asking his sister to take care of him, Zack knew that was wrong. Leah had five children of her own to raise. And besides, he didn't want to make his son feel that his father had abandoned him as well.

A whistle sounded loudly that pulled him from his thoughts.

Sweat dripped down his spine, and he winced. The train had arrived. His nerves only grew more frantic as he rubbed his hands together and then tried to wipe the damp sweat on his pants. It was a cold December day with two feet of snow. But all he could feel was a heat burning down on him.

He had to be there for her. He couldn't just tell the woman to come and then leave her stranded in a strange place. Ella would have had his head for such a cruel action.

So he would pick her up. Leah had offered to keep the girl at her place until their wedding.

A wedding. Just the thought of a second wedding made his stomach bottom out. It was hard to breathe as he tried to imagine promising himself to someone else. He wasn't certain that Ella would have wanted that. They had planned to be together for the rest of their lives. Not for only seven short years.

After he had written to Miss Della Prescott of New York City to invite her to formally join him in Montana, Zack had sent her that final letter to explain that he couldn't have another marriage like the one he had before. It would be a marriage of convenience. They would only wed when he was prepared for it, and that was only if Ross took to her. But he didn't want to rush into any commitments, and he couldn't love her like he had loved Ella.

Zack paused. No, he corrected himself. He still loved Ella. Even if she was gone.

The train had come to a stop ahead of him at the station. People were beginning to gather around. The station had been only built in the last year and stops were still rare. It was a spectacle for the town to see, though few people ever boarded the contraption from their northern town. And only a handful of people ever climbed off at their stop.

It was a sunny December Wednesday as four people stepped down from the stairs on the train platform. Zack froze as he studied each of them.

The first was an old woman with white hair who scowled at everyone except for a young woman who arrived to lead her away. The second and third were a young couple with bright red hair who hurried off through the crowd.

Then the fourth was a slim figure of a woman dressed in a dark blue traveling outfit and a dark veil. It looked like a net that tucked under her chin. She carried a bag in each hand as she shakily climbed down onto solid ground. He stood there for a minute as the figure paused and looked around. She wasn't hurrying off to greet anyone. No one was coming up to her.

Although he knew Ella was gone, he could have sworn he felt her hands on his back nudging him forward. Zack found the energy to start moving his legs toward the young lady on the other end of the platform. He pulled off his hat as he watched the veil lift and tucked over the small hat.

It wasn't a useful hat, for it hardly covered part of her head. That would never keep anyone warm. Zack then dropped his gaze to the face and paused. Blonde hair and blue eyes. A pert nose and plump lips. Then she had pale skin except for something on her cheek. At first, he thought it was a scab. When he reached her, he realized it was a birthmark.

Though he wanted to ask why she hadn't mentioned such a thing to him before, Zack was too uncomfortable to say anything besides, "Miss Prescott?" He tried to swallow the lump in his throat and was glad he hadn't eaten anything that morning. Zack wasn't certain it would have stayed down.

Her eyes widened before she nodded. "Yes. Yes, that's me. Della. Are - are you Zack Heston?"

Zack shifted uneasily. "Yes." His tongue stuck to the roof of his mouth. Dropping his gaze, he glanced at his hat in his hands. A wind chilled his ears, so he hurriedly put it back on. He dropped his eyes from her down to the ground, not knowing where to look. Not the birthmark.

Anywhere but the face. "Are those all your bags?"

When she nodded in confirmation, he grabbed them. "The wagon is this way."

She trailed behind him as he led her to the wagon. Zack ransacked his brain for words to say to her, but he couldn't think of anything. Nothing sounded right in his head. He couldn't remember being so tongue-tied around Ella.

Fortunately, his body remembered what to do. He helped the young woman into the wagon and then climbed up the other side to take the reins. Zack offered Della a short nod and then started them off down the lane. Leah would be ecstatic to have another woman around, and maybe she could help him remember how to talk to people.

But there wasn't any chance of marrying if he couldn't communicate with her.

Chapter 5

"Miss Della Prescott! Welcome, oh welcome!"

The tall woman wrapped her arms around Della before she could even react. She stopped in amazement and wondered if the woman was mad. They didn't know each other. Society always deigned an introduction. But then she remembered she was out of society and in a place she knew nothing about. When the stranger pulled back, her eyes were bright and she was smiling wide. It was hard not to like her immediately

"I'm Leah Ganey," the woman finally explained. "Zack's younger sister. We are so happy to have you here. My, you look lovely.

Please, come in. It's so cold out there. Zack, did you not have any blankets out for her? You rascal. Come in, both of you."

Della was ushered in before she had a chance to say anything. She had thought they would be wed and start their new life together. But apparently she was in someone else's home. Though she felt certain his letters had mentioned a sister, she couldn't remember anything to say. Her eyes skittered between Leah and Zack, hesitant of how to act. Everything was so new and strange. Nothing was as she had expected upon her arrival.

While she hadn't truly expected her intended would wrap his arms around her, she had hoped for a warmer reception. Zack Heston had said very little to her. While he'd been courteous enough to help with her bags in the wagon, he'd said very little.

It was the birthmark. That had to be it. She knew she should have kept her veil down a little longer. But when no one had come up to her upon leaving the train, Della thought it best she lift the veil to show the horrible defining feature so he would know who to look for. Sure enough, he immediately appeared before her. Except, he hadn't even smiled.

He hated it. A knot refused to untangle itself in her stomach. He couldn't stand her. The entire wagon ride, she could hear it in the rolling of the wheels. The man wouldn't look at her because he was disgusted with her looks. Della had to force the tears back as she wished she could do something.

There was a small scar on the edge of her birthmark where she had once taken a knife to it. Elsie had been the one to stop her. Della now wondered if she should have tried again.

She wondered what he would do. The man was so aloof that he wouldn't say a word to her after they boarded the wagon and even as he brought her up to a house. It was nice and large and wider than anything she had ever seen. To her surprise, it wasn't his house.

"Do you have all of your luggage?" Leah was asking as she brought them into the hall. "We have a room made up just for you. It's a little noisy home we have, but you're more than welcome to treat it like your own. Here, let me take that coat of yours. Is it truly velvet?"

"I, yes," Della managed shyly. "Thank you." She touched the small hat and veil hesitantly, wondering if she should drop it over her face. But it would be impolite to wear it in their house, she realized. Besides, they had already seen the birthmark by then.

Even as she took it off, a lump formed in her throat. Though she'd experienced little of society, all the proper manners had been bred into her from an early age. Especially the fact that indecent people never appeared before others to avoid any consequential concern.

Her fingers itched for the familiar netting as Leah set it aside.

Della felt naked to the soul. Clasping her hands before her, she tried to catch Zack's eye. But the man was determined to ignore her as he slowly took off his jacket.

She wished he would say something. Shame crept warmly up her cheeks. Just something, Della wished. Even if it was horrible. The silence made her too nervous.

"This way, then," Leah said after a moment of tense silence. When Della looked up, she wondered how forced the other woman's smile must be.

Voices shouting grew louder as Della wandered farther into the house. She caught a glimpse of running children before they turned into a hallway, and a door opened. Leah stepped through ushering them in. Zack followed after Leah and set her things down.

"I should go back," Zack said. "I'll drop Henry off when I pass by."

Della's heart sunk. He was going back where? It sounded like he was going to leave her there. She scrambled in her brain for something to say just as Leah addressed her. "You should walk him to the door, then come join me in the kitchen."

Not knowing what else to do, Della obeyed. Breathless, she nodded and followed him. She trailed behind Zack as he led the way to the door, hands wriggling as she tried to find something to say as he put his jacket back on.

"Thank you for the ride," she offered, hoping to earn a smile from him. Or a look. Or something.

He nodded as he finally turned around and glanced up at her. His blue eyes were shockingly icy. She could feel her entire body freeze. Della wasn't even certain if she was breathing. But there was something in his eyes that held her still, unable to do anything but focus on him. Her stomach fluttered as she found herself wanting to reach out to him to warm him up.

But then Zack looked away and left before she could take another breath.

It left her in a confused daze. Della couldn't stop thinking about him even as Leah called for her to join the family in the kitchen. Supper time had arrived without warning. It was there that she met four of the children, all but Henry who was not yet there.

Though the children stared at her in the beginning, they prioritized their food and dug in. Learning that Della was from far away, they flooded her with questions that their parents couldn't prevent. Any hesitance she'd clung to soon faded as she found herself popular with the Ganey children. They were all filled with the Christmas spirit of joy and curiosity.

Over the next couple of days, Della always had company.

The time moved along at a steady pace where there was always something to do. Her stay there was different than that of the maids who were paid to be around the house and to help her. Instead, she found herself helping the children. She was glad that they accepted her and her looks, and she was glad to be kept busy with filling Christmas stockings with gingerbread and nuts.

But every day, she turned to the window and looked for Zack.

Three days passed without him coming by, and she wondered what had happened to him. Every night, she questioned if her birthmark was truly the worst thing he had ever seen. She wondered if she would ever see him again, or if he would try to send her back to New York.

The very thought of returning made her shudder. But Della wondered how much better this life was when she still felt alone.

Chapter 6

Zack dropped Henry off outside the house and made his way back to his house with his son.

He had brought Della Prescott out there in Montana to them, but he hadn't told Ross about the young woman. He didn't know how to explain it. Part of him wondered if it would bother Ross thinking that his mother was about to be replaced. But then he had to remember how it was for Ross that he had ever put an ad out in the first place.

The unease didn't drop from his stomach.

He wondered if Della liked him. He wondered if he liked Della. He wondered what Ross would think of Della. He wondered what Della thought of Ross. Though he'd sent her that last note explaining he had a son and that it was only a marriage of convenience, he hadn't received a reply, nor had she asked about Ross earlier.

There was a world of questions in his mind as he pondered how their meeting had gone. He was still struggling to grasp the fact that she was there. Della Prescott was at his sister's house.

"How was school?" He cleared his throat and glanced over at his son.

Ross was playing with a loose thread on his mittens as he shrugged. "I don't like it. Numbers are hard, Papa. Why can't I just stay here on the ranch with you?"

That was an idea.

It was something he had considered before that point as well. Especially after Ella's passing, neither of them wanted to be far from one another. They'd spent months living alongside each other as they learned how to process their grief. Ross had become a good helping hand as a very young child. Enough so that Zack still found himself looking around for the boy while he worked most days, even after sending him to school in the mornings.

"We'll see," Zack said finally. "We'll see."

He wasn't ready to see Della Prescott anymore that night. Just meeting her had overwhelmed him. Zack took care of the horses and slumped in the kitchen as he processed his thoughts. The young woman had acted polite enough, though she was rather quiet. And young, almost ten years his junior. She looked a little frailer than he had expected, however, and the birthmark had caught him off guard.

There was nothing else that it could be. Though he hadn't seen many birthmarks, he knew they were permanent and painless and not a problem. But it could bother people. Zack wondered if it bothered Della. Burying his face in his arms at the table, he asked himself if she was the type of person that he could bring into his house forever.

The house. It needed attention. He should clean and take care of the house. While Zack understood this fact, he couldn't seem to embrace it. His thoughts were a mess, and he could hardly think about the messy state that his house was also in. He spent the evening thinking about Della Prescott.

It was too early to see if he had made the right choice.

Zack let three days pass everyone by as he mustered up the courage and willpower to return to his sister's house. Or rather, it was Henry stopping by to let them know they were being specifically invited to supper that drove him forward. After they bundled up and headed down the lane, he glanced over at Ross and managed to finally tell him what was going on.

He didn't want to. But he had to grow up sometime and play the adult.

"Your Aunt Leah," he cleared his throat, "has a guest over right now. Her name is Miss Della Prescott."

Ross glanced up from the bundle of bread they had made that day. "Miss Della? Where did she come from?"

"New York City. It's on the east coast. A - a big, popular city."

The boy nodded. "Why is she here and not in the city?"

Though he didn't want to lie, Zack wasn't certain he was ready to give his son the complete answer. They had written letters to each other about making a life together. But now that she was here, everything felt different. His stomach was constantly in knots, and he grew anxious. Zack wondered what Ella would have thought and wondered what Della was thinking. He was asking himself so many questions that he no longer knew exactly what he thought himself.

"She's just here." Zack's mouth turned dry as he tried to smile.

Ross accepted that answer. He didn't really have any other questions. And as they quickly arrived at his brother-in-law's farm, Zack brought the wagon around. "All right, let's get inside. It's going to be a cold evening."

The two of them hurried up and stepped inside.

"We're here!" Ross chorused. Boots were pulled off, along with jackets, before heading into the kitchen.

Zack stopped in the doorway when he saw Leah and Della talking together near the sink. Both women turned around. Leah beamed as Ross came over to hug her. Della studied Zack, though he couldn't read the look on her face.

"Look at you," Leah chuckled. "It's about time you came back to see us, Ross. Zack, we were wondering where you two were. And what is that you've brought?"

Ross pulled up the towel to show the bread. "Our favorite bread. We even melted butter on it. Are you the lady from the city?"

Della's eyes widened before they softened into a smile. Zack felt his shoulders tense as he watched the two interact. When Leah grabbed the bread, Della guided him off to find the children who were adding the last of the berries to their Christmas tree. They could be heard in the next room with the others, preparing for the holiday.

It wasn't until they were all seated around the supper table that the tension in his body began to loosen. Della and Ross were seated together, and he watched his son ask her question after question. Though he cut in to stop the boy, she said she didn't mind. His heart pattered as he watched them talk.

Ross liked her. He was actually talking to her. The boy had a tendency to shy away from strangers. But soon, they were nudging each other and giggling. His son grinned big with happiness shining through his eyes.

Only then did Zack contemplate that perhaps he had done the right thing by sending for Della Prescott.

Chapter 7

Della was terribly confused.

Not only did Zack leave her with these strangers, as kind and generous as they were, for several days, but then he showed up at the house with an eight-year-old son. Though their hair and eyes were different colors, the nose was too obvious to ignore.

Ross Heston was a precocious boy with a wonderful sense of humor and curiosity. He had interesting questions to ask and wanted to know about the strangest things.

But she didn't know where it came from. Della racked her brain for anything in the missives that had mentioned Zack with a son. It had never been mentioned and while the boy was sweet, she didn't like the idea that he had purposely not told her.

She had been honest about everything in her letters. Why had he chosen otherwise?

Perhaps, she had been too hasty. They had only been writing for a couple of months.

Towards the end of the supper, all six children in the house cleaned up and went off to play around the Christmas tree. This left the adults to talk, where the two men began to discuss their plans for their cattle in the next couple of months. Della used the time to think, wondering if everything she was experiencing was normal. The adjustment to seeing everything different and new in Montana felt difficult, and she worried she had been foolish. Perhaps, she was too naïve. She hadn't had enough life experiences with people and society to know how to act and behave.

"Della?"

She glanced up and forced a smile. "Sorry, Leah. I was lost in my thoughts. Yes?"

Leah held a bowl in her hands as she gestured to Zack with her elbow. "It sounds like they are leaving, so you should see them out."

Her legs obeyed, helping her to stand. "Yes, of course." She caught Zack's eye as she stepped over to him. He nodded and whistled to Ross. Soon, the three of them were crowded in the hallway.

"You should come see my horse sometime," Ross announced to Della. "Then you could ride him!"

She smiled. "That sounds lovely, Ross. But I'm afraid I don't know how to ride a horse. Thank you, though. That's very kind of you."

The little boy's bright eyes widened in disbelief. "You don't know how to ride! That's silly." She chuckled. "Papa can teach you! He taught me and now I'm really good. Right? You could teach her. Then we could all go riding. You can ride my horse, and I'll ride our pack horse. His name is Billy."

"That's a good name for a horse," Della said with a serious expression. "I look forward to that day." Her eyes flickered over to Zack, and she wondered what he thought. For a second, a dark look passed over his face. But it disappeared so quickly that she wasn't certain if she had imagined it.

Ross put on his shoes and glanced at his father. "Can we? Can we all go riding?"

Settling a hat on his head, Zack offered a hesitant nod before turning to face Della straight on. "I think that sounds like a good idea. It would be nice to show Miss Della around the property."

"Yeah!" Ross cheered.

The man studied her with a slight cock of his head. His look was so intense that Della could feel the heat climbing her cheeks. She bit her lip, hoping he wasn't thinking about her birthmark. Anything but that. There was something about the way he looked at her, though, that made her feel certain that he didn't even see it. That all he saw was her.

Della felt her heart skip a beat.

She wanted to say something but couldn't find her voice. Zack said nothing as he considered her. The more he looked at her, the more she found it impossible to look away. Tension built up between them, and it only made the thumping of her heart grow louder and louder until it was deafening.

"We should go."

Della gasped lightly for breath when Zack dropped his gaze. The man turned to open the front door in one motion. Soon, he and his son were out on the porch, leaving for the evening. They left Della in the hallway, confused over what had just happened.

That evening, she prayed for the best. But the following morning, her uncertainties and fear crept back into her mind.

Montana was beautiful. Leah and her family were polite and kind. But that wasn't why she had traveled all that way to enjoy the scenery and another's family.

***

Over the next two weeks, Zack came to two more suppers and stopped by on a few other occasions. But they were only brief visits and she rarely had a moment alone with him. It made her wonder what she had done wrong, if he had decided her birthmark was much too cumbersome to deal with. That she was too much.

The idea of returning to New York City kept her awake at night.

She shuddered and wrapped herself tight in the blankets, squeezing her eyes shut as she attempted to convince herself that she had never been a prisoner and would never be one again. But just thinking about her drab rooms and the quiet days alone bothered her.

"Della? Is everything all right?"

Blinking, she glanced around and then turned to Leah. "I'm sorry?"

The other woman leaned forward as the rest of her family ate. "You haven't touched your food. And you didn't eat earlier today, did you? You're not falling ill, are you?"

A full plate of food sat untouched before her. As everyone glanced at her, Della felt the heat climb up her cheeks. She thought fast. "Ah. Yes, I see. I mean no. No, I'm not ill. I'm just… I was thinking about the Christmas baking you were discussing yesterday."

The younger girls beamed. "Chocolates!"

Della swallowed and then smiled. "Not quite, I… My mother would host these parties and have the most incredible food. Plum pudding, roasted nuts, and even Victoria cakes."

Nodding, Leah beamed. "Wonderful. We shall make those this weekend. I wasn't thinking of cakes, but we must have them. They're one of Zack's favorites. Thank you, Della."

She nodded after picking up her fork. She had to eat something. So, she dove into the food. Then she dove into Christmas preparations with Leah. Della needed something to distract her from Zack's strange behavior. And as Ross began to visit for a few more days, she found herself developing an attachment with the boy.

It wasn't on purpose and soon, Della worried if that was a bad idea. If things didn't work out well, then it could end in heartbreak.

She didn't understand Zack and spent most nights worrying about everything going on. What was she doing there, if he had changed his mind about marrying her?

Chapter 8

"And after that," Ross explained, "Della showed me how to draw my horse. Look!"

Zack gripped the reins tightly before glancing over at the piece of paper his son pulled out. It took him two turns of the head to get a good look. There were scribbles around the page, but there was indeed a sketch of a horse on one corner of the page.

Nodding, he gave his son a grin. "That's really good, Ross. You have some talent there. Well done."

The boy beamed. "Thanks! Is she ever going to come over and visit at our house? I don't think Della goes anywhere like I do.

Maybe she would want to come to school with me and Henry. Could she come with me, Papa?"

He hesitated only a second before shaking his head. "No, Ross. She's too old for that. I think she has been to school enough."

"Oh." The boy shrugged and then hopped down once they came to a stop at their barn. "I still think she should come over. She hasn't seen my horse yet. I told her I would."

Unhitching the horses, Zack tried to imagine bringing Della over to the house. He had meant to do it at one occasion. Maybe her first week there. But she looked so comfortable at his sister's house that he didn't want to be a bother. Besides, it was easier to visit her there instead of bringing her to his house and then taking her back. That didn't make any sense to him.

So, he told Ross. "I don't know when she's coming over, Ross. Don't plan on it. Not yet, anyways."

"Then when?" the boy asked hopefully.

"I don't know," Zack repeated. He gripped the reins tightly on Billy, wishing Ross could talk about something else.

But the boy was persistent. "What about tomorrow?"

"No, Ross."

"Then Christmas?"

Zack gritted his teeth. "I don't know!" The words came out louder and harsher than he had intended. After he winced, he opened his eyes and turned to see Ross's face. His son was frozen in his tracks, eyes to the ground with a tight-lipped look like he was trying not to cry.

That was a mistake. Zack hadn't meant any of it. His heart tightened as he attempted to backtrack. But as Zack opened his mouth, he couldn't find any words. "Ross, I… that wasn't what I meant."

"I know." The words were so small in little Ross's mouth. "I'm sorry."

There was a tense silent as Zack forced himself to pull his thoughts together. "Go back to the house. You can… you can put your picture up somewhere. Any place you like. I'll take care of the horses and - and then we'll eat."

Ross turned away. "I'm not hungry." And then he hurried back to the house.

It wouldn't do him any good to follow. He had already apologized. Shaking his head, Zack went to work with the horses. Keeping his hands busy helped him to think. His thoughts wandered over to his son. He wasn't doing enough to be a good father. But he didn't know how to do any better.

That reminded him of how he wanted to get the boy a mother for the holidays. But Della was quiet, and he didn't know what to say to her. He didn't know what to do. Every time they ran into each other, he felt confused and lost. It had been a long time since he had courted someone, after all.

He was still thinking on that as he returned inside for the evening. It wasn't until he was guiding Ross to bed that the child started coughing.

"Whoa," Zack patted the boy on his back. "Are you all right? Here, under the covers. We don't want you falling ill. I'll bring you some water." When he returned, however, and touched the boy's forehead, Zack's heart thumped for another reason.

Ross was warm. Too warm. The boy shivered as he drank the chilled water. Zack ended up staying the night beside his boy, neither of them hardly sleeping.

The fever came in fast on the boy, feeding fear into Zack's heart. He had lost his wife to illness just two years prior. He wasn't about to lose his boy.

By morning, he was frantic with concern as he moved around the house and tried to take care of Ross.

When he didn't make it out on the range, his foreman came up to the ranch house to see what the problem was. Zack quickly explained the issue to Martin and then sent the man over to the next farm to retrieve Leah.

And then he resumed his pacing.

An hour later, Leah and Della arrived. The women hurried to the door, carrying blankets and towels. Zack grabbed everything he could to help them hasten, growing clumsy from his haste.

"What exactly is wrong with him?" Leah always went straight to business.

He had been practicing the words all morning but now they were gone. "He's hot. He – Ross - my boy. It's a fever, but - I don't know…" Zack didn't want to finish the words, feeling the dread cling to his spine.

It just couldn't be what had taken his wife. It couldn't be. The fear clawed at his throat as he stared at his sister desperately.

Leah brushed back her hair. She nodded to him and then nodded to Della.

"Let's see how he is. I sent Robert to retrieve Doctor Crest. Perhaps he will be able to help. Has he slept at all? Come on, then." She led the way into the house. Zack forced himself to stand back a second for Della to go before him. The young woman hesitated and then hurriedly followed after Leah, and then he brought up the rear, nearly on her heels.

"Leah! Della!" Ross sat up in his bed only to fall into a coughing fit.

Hurrying forward, Zack tried to fix the pillows and held one of his son's shoulders to try and help. Anything to help his son. Even now, he could see Ella's features in him and how the disease had taken his wife from him. He gave his sister a pained look. She had to be able to do something. The woman had her own kids and had cared for them through illnesses, hadn't she?

When she met his gaze, Leah nodded. "Della, get him comfortable, would you? I'm going to start a fire. We'll want some hot water for a bath. We can have him all cozy and clean for when the doctor arrives."

The two women started moving about to take care of everything. Zack found himself only in their way, so he passed outside in the hallway. Though he wanted to say something to Della, to at least thank her for being around to help, he couldn't find the words. The fear wouldn't let go of him. He just needed his son to be healthy again.

Chapter 9

"Thank you." Zack's voice was hoarse after he closed the door to Ross's room.

His son was finally resting. After a bath and a visit from the doctor, the young boy had finally dozed off into a fitful sleep.

When he turned around to face the ladies, his sister wrapped her arms around him. Della took a small step back and wanted to turn away so she could give them a quiet moment together. But she didn't want to wander around a house that wasn't hers. Especially one where she hadn't even been invited to yet. Not formally, at least. So she stood there, stiffly, trapped.

Leah had instructed her to come with her in the cart. Though Della had wanted to be helpful upon hearing about Ross, she worried it wasn't her place. Zack hadn't wanted her at his home, and she didn't want to be in the way. His eyes had hardly seen her when they arrived, however. She could see in his face the concern and fear for his son. Her heart went out to him as she wished she could only do more. No one deserved such trouble.

After one more squeeze, Leah stepped away. "You don't have to do it alone. Zack, we're here for you."

He nodded hesitantly. "Thank you. I - I would appreciate it."

"Doctor Crest said that Ross's fever is stabilized," Leah continued speaking. "That's good news, understand? We just need to keep an eye on him. We must make sure the fever does not grow worse, and that he has plenty of time to heal. I'd put it at about a week, all right? Now, I have to return home to tend to the children, but I can come back later."

Zack's eyes widened. Della couldn't explain the look on his face, but it made her heart break. "You'd leave?" he asked his sister hoarsely.

"No," Della jumped in before she knew what she was doing. The siblings turned to look at her as though they had just remembered they weren't alone. She didn't know what she was doing, but she couldn't let Ross suffer anymore. "I'm here. I can help." She tried to give them a smile but worried because she knew it was crooked. Her birthmark was in the way. So she stopped and ducked her head. After all, this was no time to be worrying about herself with an ailing child in the next room. "If that's all right."

"I…"

Leah jumped in. "Yes! Della, thank you. That would be perfect. Zack, I told you. We are not leaving you alone. Look at you. You're almost as exhausted as Ross. I keep telling you that you're doing too much. Now is a chance for you to rest as well."

"But…"

Though she was younger, his sister was having none of his hesitation. Della watched Leah straighten her shoulders and get to business. "We can't have you growing sick. You're going to bed now. I will return home to check on my family. Then I'll return with Robert in a few hours; he'll bring Della back to our house, and we'll switch in the morning. Della can keep an eye on Ross during the day, and I can handle him in the evening. I think that's best kept proper. Yes?"

Zack glanced between them uneasily. "If you think that's best, I suppose."

Della felt her mouth turn dry. Only now did she think of the consequences of her assistance. She would be left alone with Zack in his house. Her mother would wail. All she could wonder, however, was if he would try to talk with her at all.

But she didn't have anything to ask or any excuses to give them, so she said nothing. After they had discussed a few more details, Leah walked out the front door which left Della alone with Zack. They glanced at each other in the hallway before hurriedly dropping their gazes.

"I should…" Zack started hesitantly as though he didn't know where to go with it.

She nodded, not knowing what else to do. "Yes. Yes, right. I'll be with Ross if you need anything."

He went down to one door, and she returned to Ross's room.

The evening passed slowly and quietly. When Leah returned to take her place, Della didn't even see Zack. When she gathered the courage to ask Robert about him on the quiet ride back to the Ganey's ranch, she learned that Zack had lost his first wife to influenza. Robert tried to speak positively about his brother-in-law, but Della found herself wondering about the man. She thought she would know the man in the letters she wrote, but she wasn't so certain anymore. Zack hardly looked at her, let alone talked to her. The man was troubled, and she worried she wasn't helping him.

***

When Della returned in the morning to take care of Ross, she was determined to focus on the boy. Ross was the one she could help. And he was the one who didn't stare at the little nightmare trapped on her cheek. Though she ran into Zack a few times, especially as she helped prepare food in the kitchen, they had little to say. The man was restless and tired himself. She could often hear him pacing nearby.

Della again focused on Ross. Within a few days, he was recovering well enough to take a walk around the house.

She cheered loudly, clapping her hands. "Wonderful! You see, Ross? You can do anything you put your mind to. Now I think we shall have supper at the supper table. How does that sound?"

"But it's fun eating in bed," he said. But he had a big grin on his face as he said it.

Chuckling, she shook her head. "Nonsense. You said just yesterday how nice it would be to return out there. Now, take a seat. I'll switch out your sheets and blankets. We'll settle you back in bed, and I'll fetch you when the soup is ready."

"I like your soup," Ross grinned. "It's really good." Then he glanced around the room as he fiddled with the blanket she had wrapped tightly around him. "Then… can we do something after supper?"

Della dropped her folded arms as she studied him curiously. "I suppose. It depends on what you want. What is it, Ross?"

He shyly glanced around before pointing across the room. There was a tree nearly her height in the corner. She wasn't certain if it had been there all along for the past couple of days or if she merely hadn't noticed it. The holidays had been far from her mind lately.

Della turned back to Ross who asked her, "Can we decorate it? Together?"

Though her eyes widened, she tried not to react. It was a simple invitation, but the way Ross phrased it made her wonder. Perhaps he was scared she wouldn't want to. After all, usually it was the children who decorated the trees.

Della smiled. She had always loved decorating for Christmas. For the past couple of years, she had tended to that duty with the maids. "I would love to, Ross. That's an excellent idea. How about this? You get some good rest, and I'll find some things we can decorate the tree with."

The boy nodded furiously. It was so fast she almost worried his head would fall off.

She chuckled and ushered the boy off to bed. Once he was under clean covers, she told him stories of New York until he fell asleep. Only then did she leave his side to tend to the kitchen while checking on him every couple of minutes.

Chapter 10

Zack tried to run his ranch, but Martin sent him back home every day.

"I have everything handled," the older man would remind him pointedly. "It's a slow season, and you should spend more time with your boy. You need the rest. You deserve it. Now get out of here before I drag you back."

He returned to the house every time.

Except during the day, Della was there. She treaded so quietly that he hardly ever heard her passing or behind him. They said little to each other and any conversation focused on Ross. His son; his boy who was the only reminder of his late wife.

At night, he would dream of her. It was always the same. Ella was weak, wasted away by her illness, and reaching out to him. But he could never reach her. He hadn't been able to save her. He had failed her.

One night after dozing in his room for a couple of blurry hours, Zack walked out into the hall to find a plate of food waiting for him on the kitchen table. His stomach growled as a reminder that he hadn't eaten all day. He took a step towards the food only to hear laughter ring out.

He paused, wondering if he was imagining things.

Then there was a giggle. Ross's giggle.

His heart skipped a beat in hope to hear that sound again. It had been too long. Though the boy had tried to laugh a few times in the past week, it always ended in a deep cough. But now, there was nothing. Zack ran across the room eagerly, into the front room where he found Della and Ross together.

The tree had been set up two weeks ago. Zack had taken Ross into the nearby mountains to find the right tree. They had waded through the snow for two hours before finding the right one. It was a thick tree, fairly small, but perfect for a young boy. They had put off decorating it, just like they had for the last couple of years. Especially after Ross had fallen sick, Zack worried that their trip had been what caused the illness. He had even considered getting rid of it so he wouldn't have to look at the bitter reminder.

Now, there were bowls of ribbons and dried fruit and pinecones everywhere, along with string. Della was telling Ross a story about leeches that made him giggle. The bottom half of the tree was looking well decorated and colorful. There were candles lit around the two of them, creating a cheerful scene.

It made his heart hurt. Only a few years ago, Ross had been doing that very thing with his mother.

It was Ella's tradition. She loved decorating the Christmas tree. The first year they were married, he had tried to help her, but he had only dropped and broken everything that he touched. She had instructed him to watch from the chair. Feeling useless, Zack would bring out his old violin and play for her.

His violin. Zack wondered where that instrument had gone. He couldn't recall the last time he had touched it. There had been one time when Ella had recently fallen ill, he recalled, where she had asked him to play for her. He had done so for hours, playing even after she had fallen asleep.

Beyond that, he couldn't recall anything. He didn't know what had happened to it or where it had gone.

Zack could feel an itch in his fingers, ready to pluck those strings.

But he didn't. Because it made him think of his wife who was no longer there with him. With them. A lump formed in his throat. He tried not to feel the pain as he watched Ross with Della. Quietly, he took a step back and then another, meaning to leave them.

Then Della started to hum. "Morning stars are growing light, let's say farewell unto the night," she leaned down and ruffled Ross's hair who stared at her in amazement. "And sing in joy for all is well."

"My mother used to sing that for me," Ross murmured. "How did you know?"

Della hummed a few more notes as Zack wondered the same question. She took her time answering before she said, "I didn't. My cook used to sing it for me when I was scared. Now, whenever I am happy or want to be happy, I think of that lullaby."

Ross handed her something that sparkled in the light. "Are you happy now?"

"I am," she assured him.

"Me too," the boy said before she could ask him.

He could hardly breathe as he heard the exchange. It took him several minutes before he mustered up the strength to turn away. Zack returned to the kitchen and quietly ate the food. Only when Ross came running in to find a glass of water did they realize he was there. He gathered the energy to help clean up the house, and then sent Ross to bed.

Zack was looking through his closet when he heard the nearby door open and close. He couldn't hear the footsteps, so he knew it was Della. Ross must have fallen asleep, and she would be preparing to leave. He tried not to think about her as he searched. But he couldn't find his violin and eventually walked out to find Della looking out a window.

"Is Leah coming?" He mustered the courage to talk to her.

The young woman jumped lightly, putting a hand over her heart as she turned back to him.

"Oh, Zack. It's you. I... I would assume so. Robert had to drive into town this morning, I believe, so they might have fallen behind. But they'll be here soon." She tried to smile. "You look better rested."

He managed a smile as he joined her at the window. But he didn't know what to say. He wasn't sure he felt well rested. Though his panic over his son had faded, there was still a sense of unease. Zack glanced back around the room as his eyes fell on the tree. It was completely decorated now, just as it should be.

"Thank you."

Della turned to him with her brow furrowed. "For what?"

It took all of his courage to speak. "For taking care of Ross. You have done a lot this week. A lot. And I am very grateful to you for it." His tongue felt thick and too big for his mouth as he talked. Zack forced himself to meet her gaze. That much he could do.

Her cheeks flushed as their eyes met. "Oh. It's all right. I'm only glad I could be of service. Ross is a wonderful boy. You - you've raised him well." She spoke softly with her sweet accent. His eyes studied the blush that crept across her face.

Zack hadn't given her a good look for a while. He wasn't sure why.

The young woman was beautiful. Though he thought he had noticed her pretty face upon her arrival, now he wasn't so certain. She had a sweet little nose and full lips with sparkling eyes. The birthmark didn't change anything, not really. Della was truly beautiful.

Swallowing hard, he forced himself to look away. He didn't want to be caught staring. Besides, he didn't know what else to say. So he gave her a nod and left the room.

Chapter 11

"Oh, you'll love it," Leah assured Della as she pulled out a bonnet. "Ah, here you go. This should fit you well."

It was a lovely bonnet with a fine trim. Though not quite as nice as something her mother would approve of, Della knew it fit well in the wild landscape of Montana. She gently ran a finger over the lace as she offered Leah a hesitant smile. "Thank you, but I'm not so certain. What if your foreman needs something?"

The Sabbath had arrived again. For the past two Sundays, there had been enough of a reason not to attend church. She had yet to explore town and though she was curious about Dawson, Della knew that people would be even more curious about her. The very idea of people staring made her stomach queasy.

But now, Leah was insisting she join them. After all, it was about time she went somewhere else between the two ranches. Now that Ross was in much better health, there weren't any other excuses keeping her out of town. At least, not that Della could convince the woman.

"Daniel?" Leah chuckled. "Of course he won't. He knows we are attending church. Besides, it's his job to take care of everything. Don't you want to join us? It's the last sermon before Christmas this week."

They would stare. People always stared. She was certain that even some of Leah's family had stared before forcing themselves to look away. Her hand raised up to pull on her hair in the hopes of hiding the birthmark.

"I don't want to cause a commotion," Della mumbled thickly with her eyes downcast.

Leah scoffed. "Unless you trip and bring the roof down, I think you're fine. It's winter, dear. Everyone will be worrying about themselves. And it's Christmas, so people are much too distracted to care if you break something. Why do you think you would cause a commotion otherwise?"

The woman had her hands on her hips with a stern expression when Della looked up. She opened her mouth to explain, but it couldn't be more obvious. Of course Leah saw the birthmark. It couldn't be ignored. They had spent weeks together. But, Della realized, the woman didn't care.

Her heart thumped loudly against her ribcage as she realized how kind Leah truly was.

It was a sweet enough notion of feeling seen that she could feel her eyes beginning to mist. Della turned away and put the bonnet on. She needed a moment to gather her emotions. Once the bonnet was on, she managed a smile back at Leah.

"To church?"

The other woman chuckled as she looped their arms. "To church."

Though Leah clearly didn't care or stare, Della noticed others studying her as they entered the small church building. She ducked her head in the hopes of not seeing everyone. But she could still feel the stares all itchy across her spine.

"Della!"

She jerked her head up to find Ross racing down the aisle to her. Her heart immediately lightened as she opened her arms to welcome him into a tight hug. The boy appeared in much better health, and he was dressed in his Sunday best. The boy looked charming, and he gripped her tight to show he had all his strength back. It made her heart glad, and she couldn't resist kissing the top of his head.

When she glanced up, she caught sight of Zack. He was staring at them with a strange look in his eyes. A flush crept up her cheeks as she slowly let go of Ross. She hoped he didn't mind. Ross was a darling boy, and it was impossible not to adore him. Especially after spending days together. Both of them craved something more, she realized, and they couldn't help but to bond.

"It is so very good to see you," she assured him but then gestured to his father. "We're about to start, and I think you should return to your father."

"Will I see you at family supper tonight?" he asked her hopefully.

She pinched his cheek teasingly. "Only if you can find me."

He scampered off, and she joined Leah with her family at their usual seats. The sermon began but Della's mind wandered. Leah and little Ross had welcomed her from the beginning in Dawson. They were kind, generous, and liked her for who she was.

Was it enough?

The doubts continued to grow, settling in a heavy pit in her stomach. Even the hymns couldn't help her feel better. Della worried that coming out west had been a mistake. Everyone liked her but the one person who was supposed to want her there the most.

Zack hardly talked to her and when he did, it was hardly about the two of them.

Besides, it was clear his missives had not been honest. He hadn't told her about his late wife and sweet child. After she had been painfully honest, it hurt that he thought it was fine to lie to her like that.

It wasn't that he was cruel. It was that she felt that she hardly existed around him. That reminded her of her parents, and that worried her. While Della didn't want to return to New York City in the safe little prison that her parents had created, Montana wasn't feeling like the freedom she had been looking for.

Chapter 12

Zack found his gaze continually drifting over to Della during church.

He hadn't expected to see her. Leah had made mention that Della didn't like going into town. It wasn't that he was avoiding her, but it was unexpected. Even more unexpected when Ross suddenly let go of his hand to run to the young woman.

Her arms had opened immediately for his son who had practically jumped into them. She'd had to take a step back to keep her balance. When most children did such a thing, Zack wanted to smile because of the unadulterated joy he knew they were experiencing. But he hadn't expected Ross to do that with Della. Then when she kissed Ross's head, all he could picture was his late wife, Ella. There were so many things the two women had in common. A strong heart, kindness, and love for Ross.

Strange emotions made his chest tighten as he tried to think about what to do or even say to her.

Instead, when Ross returned to his side, they went to their seats.

Though he had wanted to give his son a mother for Christmas, Zack was only growing more anxious about the idea. He hardly knew Della and there had been too much going on. He thought of Ella and wondered what she would think. What she would do.

But thinking of her only made his heart hurt.

Zack dropped his head in his hands as the sermon continued. He searched his heart for the truth, seeking to better understand what he was doing and what he needed to do. Though he hadn't promised Della marriage, for there hadn't been a proposal, he hadn't planned for not marrying her.

Was that an option? He wasn't certain. It only prompted guilt and discomfort as he thought about telling her to leave.

After the closing prayer, Zack was one of the first people to stand up. "Let's go," he told Ross. "We'll see your Aunt Leah and the others tonight. I want to check in on the ranch. We should leave now."

Ross nodded, picking up his hat and making their way into the aisle. Everyone joined there as well, so it was difficult to make their way through the crowd. He grabbed hold of his son's hand and nodded to the people he recognized.

"Annabeth," someone said next to him, "It's so good to see you again." Everyone talked and chattered away as he walked.

"I can hardly believe the weather these days. It's been so cold."

"That was such a lovely sermon, wasn't it?"

"We're looking for our daughter, you see. She disappeared."

One voice stood out, though he didn't know why. He didn't recognize the voice. But then he realized he had recognized the accent. It was similar to Della's New York accent. When they neared the back of the church, he paused to look around.

Leah had her family gathered in the front of the church, talking to Nancy Heim, the pianist. Robert was the only one not in their group, for he was talking to the Calhoun family who ran the haberdashery. There were other familiar faces in the crowd as well.

His gaze fell upon someone who looked like Della. Zack blinked. But it wasn't Della. It was an older woman who had the same hair, all pinned up. The woman was refined and looked out of place in Montana. He assumed she was the one with the similar accent and wondered if Della knew them.

"Papa?"

Ross's voice pulled him from the daze. Zack shook his head and then turned to his son.

"Right. Let's go home." He cleared his throat as they made their way home. Ross had toys to play with as Zack went out to check on his men and his cattle. They had things under control, of course, but it was good to spend some time with everyone.

And as usual, he grabbed Ross and they made their way over to the Ganey ranch for Sunday supper. They had missed it the week before with Ross's ailment, but hopefully now, life could go back to normal. As they stepped inside his sister's house, he could smell the roast cooking.

Ross ran down the hall, and Zack followed after him.

"Come in," Leah called to them. "You're nearly late. We're about to say grace."

Zack obeyed and found everyone seated. He took the seat beside his son and across from Della. After a short nod to her, he gave another nod to his sister who quieted everyone to say grace. Everyone then dug in cheerfully, talking and enjoying their food.

"Victoria cake!" Ross announced excitedly when dessert came around. "That's my favorite!"

Henry laughed beside him. "And mine!"

"And Papa's," Ross added as he passed the platter to Zack. He grinned at his boy and nodded. If he hadn't had his fork readily available, Zack was certain Ross would have dug in with his hands. "Mmm! They're just like Mama's. She makes them just like this. Well, she used to," he added softly.

When he glanced over, Zack tried to give his son a smile. He patted him on his shoulder but couldn't muster up the words. Ross was right. Everyone in town knew about the way Ella could make the perfect Victoria cake. People asked her to make it all the time. And he could never get enough of it.

"That's very sweet," Leah broke in gently. "And correct. Ross, Ella made wonderful cakes. We thought it was time to enjoy the cake again. Della was kind enough to make it for us."

Ross bounced in his seat. "Della, you made this? It's really good. Papa, can Della be my new mother?"

His head jerked up in surprise. Zack felt his stomach drop. Though he wanted to think of something to say, Zack had no words. He glanced at Della who looked at him through wide eyes.

Blinking, Zack glanced at his son and then at his sister. "If you'll excuse me," he choked out.

Then he left the table.

When Leah found him on the back porch, she handed him his jacket. "That wasn't very polite," she told him.

"I know," he scowled. He had realized his mistake but there was nothing he could do about it now. He had made too many mistakes lately and it seemed impossible to resolve them. The lump in his throat hadn't gone away, and he couldn't bring himself to return inside.

She put out an arm, but he walked around her. His sister huffed. "He's just a boy. Of course he has feelings. That wasn't meant to hurt you. But you know Della and Ross deserve an answer to that question, don't you?"

He stopped to give her a look. "I can't." It took all his strength to keep his voice from breaking. "It was a mistake. I should have never sent for Della."

Leah licked her lips as she appeared to think for a minute. Then she squeezed his arm. "Even after everything? She came all this way. I know she cares for you and Ross." His sister hesitated. "I won't tell you what to do. Only that it's been two years, Zack. You're only hurting yourself more by not letting go. Do you understand?"

He inhaled sharply and shrugged. It didn't matter. He had made up his mind.

Chapter 13

Christmas Eve was a wonderful morning where everyone played. There was music and dancing and games. Della hadn't enjoyed an occasion like it since she and her siblings were young and still had enough to do around the house. Before they had gone out into society.

It made for a bittersweet day. Between all the fun, she thought of her family.

Hopefully, they were well. She thought about the letter she had left behind. It had been short, only telling everyone that she was safe where she was going. She wanted to live her life in freedom and joy in a way she had not been able to do for the last twenty-three years. She didn't want to be a burden, and she didn't want to feel like a prisoner.

Though she loved them and wished them well, she knew her way of life had not been desirable. Living confined was not the way for anyone to live.

Everyone settled around for an early supper. The children had been practicing their speaking in school recently and wanted to put on a small reenactment of the nativity. It would be the show of the evening, and they were all buzzing around excitedly.

As she sat down, however, she noticed two plates were not set for Zack and Ross. She glanced around hesitantly before clasping her hands together. Henry was just arguing with his littlest sister, Lacy, when there was a knock at the door.

Her heart skipped a beat. Had Ross and Zack come to join them?

But then she was reminded that the table was full. She glanced over at Leah and Robert who shrugged to one another. They didn't know who it was. Whoever was at the door had not been expected.

"I'll get it!" Henry jumped up and ran off.

"Then I get to say grace," Lacy exclaimed, clapping her hands together.

"Hush," Leah quieted her children as she followed Henry. She paused at the end of the table as they heard the door open.

Henry spoke loudly for everyone to hear. "Hello! Merry Christmas Eve. I'm Henry. Welcome to the Ganey household. What can we do for you?"

Della couldn't help but smile at how well he spoke. She was about to comment to Leah and Robert, but the next voice she heard made her freeze in her chair.

"It's a pleasure to meet you, young man."

There might have been something said after that, but Della stood up so quickly that her chair fell over behind her. It echoed in her ears as she questioned herself that she might be dreaming.

But if she was, how was she to wake up?

"Father?" Her brow furrowed as she murmured the name softly.

But it couldn't be. She was a world away from them. There was no way they could find her. Unless, of course, Hazel had said something. Della put a hand to her stomach as it began to churn uneasily. Her feet led her around the table and down the hall. She couldn't help herself. She had to make sure she wasn't imagining his voice.

When Della stepped into the hall, however, she found her parents.

Donald was still tall with his shoulders thrown back. And Judy still looked like the beautiful socialite she had been raised to become. She stared incredulously, wondering how they had come so far. Why were they there?

Her question was answered as her mother cried out. Clasping a hand over her mouth, the older woman swept over and pulled Della into a tight hug. A soft sob escaped just as Della watched her father follow closely behind to sweep them into his arms. She couldn't move, frozen in confusion.

"We've been looking everywhere for you, young lady," he announced to her.

Through her bleary tears, Judy explained. "Everywhere, Della. I was so worried! Why did you leave us like that?"

"I…" Della hesitated as they pulled away.

She glanced around as Leah grabbed Henry's arm in the doorway. She gave a quick nod to Della, and they disappeared to give her privacy.

She swallowed as she turned back to her parents. "I told you. I wanted my freedom. I didn't want to be hidden away anymore."

Her mother tugged her into another hug, nearly pulling her off her feet. "Oh darling! You were never a burden. We had no idea you felt that way until your letter. We were only trying to protect you. That's all. Had we known… I never wanted to drive you away."

She was stunned as her mother kissed her cheek and hugged her tightly once more. Her eyes fell upon her father who nodded. The man looked like he was trying to hold back tears. He had never cried before. It was the most bewildering reunion she could ever imagine. But the knot in her stomach began to loosen.

Not certain of what else to do, Della sat with her parents and caught up with them.

They wanted her home. They wanted her as part of their family. And they would give her anything to know she could do whatever she wished. It was a misunderstanding that had never been made clear. Della's heart grew light as she learned the truth. They were only trying to protect her. All three of them apologized, lightening the loads on their heavy hearts.

Afterward, Della introduced her parents to the Ganey family who invited her parents to join them for supper. More space was set up around the table, and everyone enjoyed a hearty meal. Della found joy in her heart and only wished that her final confusing relationship could be cleared up.

She had only told them the smallest details about her relationship. And when they asked, she simply told them that they were still unwed, and he lived nearby. Much more in her life was finally making sense. All except for Zack Heston. As she glanced at her parents, she wondered what might happen next.

Chapter 14

It was Christmas tradition to take an evening ride around the ranch.

Zack could hardly believe it was Christmas Eve again. Time was flying by and soon, his son would be a man. He glanced over at Ross who looked around with a serious expression. Mountains descended upon them within the next couple of miles, and everything was wrapped in a cold layer of snow.

"Ross?" The boy was too sober for a boy of his age. "What's on that mind of yours?"

He slowed down when Ross didn't respond. The boy shrugged and then darted a hesitant look over. Whatever it was, he didn't want to say it. "Nothing."

"Oh really?" Zack chuckled, feeling lighthearted for once. "Somehow, I doubt that."

Ross shrugged again. "It's only… I guess I thought Della came here to have Christmas with us. I thought she was my present. But Uncle Rob said maybe not, and I shouldn't talk to you about it."

The lightness in his chest tightened. He had forgotten how perceptive Ross could be as a child. A lump formed in his throat. He searched for the right words to explain. "It's not that. I only… I don't know if she's right for us."

"But I like her," Ross mumbled. "And she said she likes me."

They fell quiet, and Zack couldn't help as his thoughts turned to the young woman.

She was pretty, he knew that. She was also smart and kind, which was obvious from their time together and as she had cared for Ross. It made his stomach queasy again just thinking about her. He couldn't explain the feeling, and it had been a long time since he had felt like this so much. Was it the winter? The cold? The food?

Then Zack realized he hadn't felt queasy like that since Ella.

His heart pounded in his chest as he thought about the young lady who had looked for him and watched him curiously whenever they were together. She would smile at him. And it was clear she adored Ross. Della was so good with him, patient and cheerful.

She was cheerful. And wise, from everything Ross had said.

The truth slowly began to dawn on him.

As they made their way quietly back to the house, Zack realized he had been wrong about everything from the beginning. He had been drowning in fear all along of embracing something new. It was easier to deal with the miserable life he already knew than embrace someone to replace his Ella.

But what would Ella think?

Even as he asked the question, he recalled one of the last conversations they'd had together. Ella had been in and out of consciousness, clutching his hands with the last of her strength. She had begged him to carry on, to be happy, if anything happened. He could hear her voice now, reminding him of this.

How had he forgotten?

"Papa?" They had reached the house, but he was still sitting atop his horse.

Zack blinked and turned to his son, stunned over his realization. "Yes?"

"Do you like Della?"

"Yes." The word slipped out before he could help himself. And as he said it, Zack knew it was true. He thought back to their missives about how sweet she was, how she craved a life out of the city. She wanted to find a new home, and he had told her he would help her.

And all he had done so far was let her be at his sister's house. He was a fool.

"I have to see her." Zack swung his horse around.

Ross hollered that he was coming. Zack rushed them the two miles between the ranches as he thought more and more about Miss Della Prescott. He thought of her sweet nature in caring for Ross, and how natural she had looked in their house. He recalled watching her decorate their Christmas tree and read stories to Ross. He thought of her at the kitchen table and remembered the strange knots in his stomach.

He had always assumed they meant everything was wrong, but he had misinterpreted them. He realized that now as he swung off his horse in the yard and helped Ross down. As he discovered the truth, he felt a weight slip off his shoulders. Zack could only hope now that Della would forgive him for his ignorance.

Together, they barged into the house as his sister's family finished singing a Christmas carol.

Breathless, Zack pulled his hat off as he looked around the parlor. Every seat was full. His sister and her family sat around cheerfully. Two strangers who looked vaguely familiar sat in chairs. And beside them was Della.

When his eyes fell on her, he could feel the pounding in his heart start up all over again.

"Della," he managed breathlessly.

She had the sweetest face. It reminded him of the mornings when she came over to visit Ross who always clapped for her. Even then, as he tried to collect his thoughts, Zack watched his son cross the room and tug Della up onto her feet. She glanced between the boys as she smiled nervously. But there was still that sparkle.

It was a Christmas miracle, he decided, the unconditional love she had shown his son. He only wished he had realized that sooner. But now, he had a chance to fix it.

"Hello, Zack. Is everything all right?"

"I'm in love with you."

Everyone stared. Zack didn't know what had compelled him to say it like that. But it was too late to take it back. He tried to smile as she stared in surprise. "I haven't showed it well, but that's because I didn't realize it until now. After our missives and your arrival and how you took care of Ross, I… I couldn't do anything else. I still don't understand it, and I might need more time, but I do. Inside and out. I don't know why it took this long, and I don't know why you didn't tell me about that mark, but it doesn't matter. I love you."

She started to smile and then paused. "But I did, Zack. I wrote you a whole letter about it… And I don't… what changed? I mean, you didn't tell me about Ross in your missives, and I haven't…"

He shook his head. "But I did. I sent it after my invitation."

Her brow furrowed for a minute before she started to laugh. Della covered her mouth as she crossed the room to him. "Then our correspondences must have been lost. No matter. That… none of that matters." She took a deep breath and then smiled hopefully. "You may take your time, as long as you need it. I'll wait here for you."

When he took Della in his arms a second later, Zack was amazed at how right it felt. Just as he mustered up the courage to kiss her, however, Ross started to cheer. The two of them jumped as they remembered they weren't alone.

Everything followed in a rush. Leah joined the cheer with laughter. The whole room brightened up at the news that Della was staying.

Zack learned that the strangers were Della's parents who had hoped to take her back to New York City.

Zack thought he would worry about that later. Della had promised to give him time.

However, by the following morning, his heart had lightened so much that before their noonday meal, he took Donald and Judy Prescott aside to ask for their blessing to marry Della. They agreed only after he promised to wait until June when they could visit again.

"What are you doing in June?" Zack asked when he pulled Della for a walk after the children had opened all their gifts. He'd had an early talk with his son, and everything was falling into place. Though it intimidated him to move so quickly, everything felt right.

Della cocked her head, her eyes tracing his features. "June? I'm not certain. Why?"

He stepped forward. "Because I think that will be enough time. And your parents said they'd be here."

"Here?" She turned from him, but he grabbed her hand. "For what? These are all riddles… unless… Is this your idea of a proposal?"

Stepping forward, Zack managed a grin. "It's been a few years since I had to do this. But yes. I want to marry you in June. I want us to have a life together. Ross loves you, and so do I. We didn't have the strongest start, but I'm ready to make up for that. Will you have me?"

She took a deep breath as she looked through wide eyes. Della had the prettiest eyes he had ever seen. All he wanted to do was take her face in his hands and study her for the rest of his life. It was the strangest feeling, but he didn't want it to end.

"Yes," Della beamed. "I will."

Zack almost laughed in disbelief. Everything had changed so quickly. The grief he had been buried in no longer felt so heavy. He felt like he could almost dance. Instead, he wrapped his arms around Della. It was only the second time he had done so, and Zack was ready for a lifetime of doing so. And finally, he kissed her.

The End

More Books by Stella Clark

The Doctor's Pregnant Bride
The Orphan Bride
The Rancher's Bride
The Preacher's Bride
The Jilted Bride
The Damaged Bride
The Widowed Bride
The Unexpected Bride
Deceiving the Bride
The Miner's Bride
The Scarred Bride
Montana Christmas Bride
Tyler's Christmas Bride

Printed in Dunstable, United Kingdom